God's Big Plan

God's
BIG
Plan

Written by
Elizabeth F. Caldwell and Theodore Hiebert

Illustrated by
Katie Yamasaki

flyaway books

How did we get to be so different?
Why do people speak so many different languages?
Wouldn't it be easier if we were all alike?

This is the story of the people of God
found in the book of Genesis—
people who were all alike
and liked it that way.
Then, God surprised them.

When the world started again after the flood, the children, grandchildren, and great-grandchildren of Noah and Naamah and all their descendants moved to a place called Shinar.

Everyone in this very large family spoke the same language and lived together in the same place.

Because they wanted this to be their home for a long time, they began to build a city. They made bricks out of mud and straw and baked them in furnaces until they were hard. They used hot tar for cement to hold the bricks together.

They said to each other, "Let's build a very big city with very tall buildings. Shinar will be home for us."

"If we build a big city with a very tall building, then we can stay together. This building will be so tall that its top will be in the clouds. It will scrape the sky! Our city and our skyscraper will keep us together forever."

They liked living together in a city where everyone knew one another. They liked speaking the same language. They liked being all the same.

God saw them building their city so that they could all stay in one place. God listened to them all talking in the same language. And God said, "If I don't do something, everyone will be just like everyone else forever."

God had a different idea—a plan for the world
to be full of many kinds of people.

First, God gave them different languages to speak.

Then, God sent them out to live throughout the whole earth.

Because God gave them different languages to speak and different places to live, they didn't finish building their city. If they had, they could have called it Manytown, because that is where the many languages of the world began.

Instead, they called that city Babel, because that was their word for dividing one language into many.

Just as God created the earth with many different
fish, birds, and animals . . .

and just as God created many
different things that grow
and live on the earth . . .

so God created people.

We speak many different languages.

We move about in many different ways.

We eat different
kinds of bread.

We eat in many different ways.

We live nearly everywhere on earth.

We come together to worship in many different places.

The people who were building Babel had a little plan to stay together. But God had a bigger plan.

God wanted to fill the world with different languages,
different people, and different ways of living.

And that's what God did.

A Note for Parents and Educators

Children grow up meeting many different people. At their lunch tables at school, Jewish, Protestant, Catholic, and Muslim students may eat together. Perhaps they learn about the ways that others worship. They may have friends from different racial or ethnic backgrounds. Together on the soccer field, children born in Myanmar, Africa, Mexico, and the United States may all learn how to kick the ball. All this wonderful difference is part of God's plan for God's world.

That's the message of the story of Babel in Genesis 11:1–9. However, its interpreters throughout history have read this story in a way that presents difference as a problem. They believed, incorrectly, that Babel's tower symbolized human pride and challenged God's rule. As a result, God's multiplying languages and dispersing people were considered a punishment for pride. Through this lens, the world's cultural diversity is God's penalty for sin.

God's Big Plan retells the story of Babel based on new scholarship that challenges this negative history of interpretation. It offers a more accurate translation of the original text for a precise reading that is more faithful to the aim of the original storyteller. The people act not out of pride, which is nowhere mentioned in the story, but to preserve their uniformity. The world's people, all speaking the same language, build their city and its tower so that they can stay in one place and keep from being spread across the earth. God sees the people's attempt to stay the same, and God responds by introducing new languages and dispersing the people. This introduction of difference is not God's punishment, a word that does not appear in the story. Instead, it is the way God intended the world to look. According to this new view, the world's cultural diversity is the plan God had for the world all along.

This story helps children see that God designed the world for all creation and all people to flourish with difference, even when people sometimes wish to build walls of homogeneity and sameness. This new/old way of telling the story is a promising way of teaching children about diversity today, which is God's gift to us all.

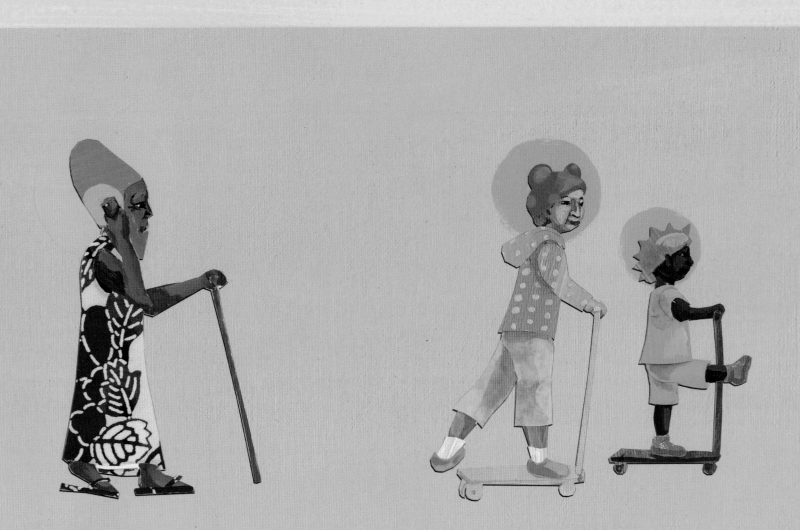

As you read this story with a child, take note:

A Story in Two Parts: The first part retells the story in the spirit of its first storyteller in Genesis 11:1–9. The second part then invites children to engage the concept of difference with things they know: animals, plants, food, people, places for worship. These common items in the lives of children will help them connect God's plan for the world with our part in living with difference.

Names: Babel is the Hebrew name of the ancient city of Babylon. In the Akkadian language of the Babylonians, *Babel* may have meant "gate of god" (*bab*: gate, *el*: god). The Hebrew storyteller connected the name Babel with the Hebrew word *balal*, "mix," giving Babel a new meaning as the place where the world's languages were mixed or multiplied. Naamah is the name we have given Noah's wife, although she is not named in the Bible. In doing this, we are following the practice of the early rabbis who gave her this name, which means "pleasant, delightful" (*Genesis Rabba* 23:3). In her book *A Prayer for the Earth: The Story of Naamah, Noah's Wife*, Sandy Eisenberg Sasso tells Namaah's story.

Illustrations: Invite children to notice what they see in the pictures. One notable detail is that the artist, Katie Yamasaki, has placed halos around the heads of the characters. She did this to symbolize their common language and sameness. Notice how she pictures sameness at the beginning of the biblical story and then how she portrays difference as the story continues.

Questions for Conversation:

1. Why do you think the people who lived in Shinar wanted to stay together?

2. What do you think happened after God sent them to different places in the world?

3. Who do you know who is very different from you? What makes you different? What makes you alike?

4. Why do you think God designed a world with so many differences in it?

We are grateful to have taught together at McCormick Theological Seminary,
a diverse community of learners and teachers. There we experienced all the beauty
and difference that God has imagined for our world. We dedicate this book to our children,
grandchildren, nieces, and nephews who we hope will continue the work of making
this world a place where everyone is welcomed into God's big family.
—E. F. C. and T. H.

For my mother, Maria. Thank you for opening the door to my journey of knowing God. I love you.
—K. Y.

Text © 2019 Elizabeth F. Caldwell and Theodore Hiebert
Illustrations © 2019 Katie Yamasaki

First edition
Published by Flyaway Books
Louisville, Kentucky

19 20 21 22 23 24 25 26 27 28–10 9 8 7 6 5 4 3 2 1

Book design by Allison Taylor
Text set in Chaparral Pro

Library of Congress Cataloging-in-Publication Data
Names: Caldwell, Elizabeth, 1948- author. | Yamasaki, Katie, illustrator.
Title: God's big plan / Elizabeth F. Caldwell and Theodore Hiebert ;
   illustrated by Katie Yamasaki.
Description: First edition. | Louisville, KY : Flyaway Books, 2019. |

Identifiers: LCCN 2018036655 (print) | LCCN 2018051093 (ebook) | ISBN
   9781611649185 (ebook) | ISBN 9781947888067 (hbk.)
Subjects: LCSH: Babel, Tower of--Juvenile literature. | Ethnicity--Religious
   aspects--Christianity--Juvenile literature.
Classification: LCC BS1238.B2 (ebook) | LCC BS1238.B2 C35 2019 (print) | DDC
   222/.1109505--dc23
LC record available at https://lccn.loc.gov/2018036655

PRINTED IN CHINA

Most Flyaway Books are available at special quantity discounts when
purchased in bulk by corporations, organizations, and special-interest groups.
For more information, please e-mail SpecialSales@flyawaybooks.com.